This book belongs to

Alana

D0297447

Characters (in order of appearance)
Narrator — Stephanie Stearns
Troy Bolton — Zac Efron and Drew Seely
Coach Jack Bolton — Bart Johnson
Mrs Montez — Socorro Herrera
Gabriella Montez — Vanessa Anne Hudgens
Ms Darbus — Alyson Reed
Sharpay Evans — Ashley Tisdale
Chad Danforth — Corbin Bleu
Kelsi Nielsen — Olesya Rulin

Read-Along Produced by Randy Thornton and Ted Kryczko
Engineered by Jeff Sheridan
Additional Engineering by Dan Montes
Read-Along Adaptation by Greg Dobrin
Based on the Disney Channel original film
Executive Producers: Kenny Ortega, Bill Borden and Barry Rosenbush

Songs:
Start of Something New
Written by Matthew Gerrard and Robbie Nevil
© 2005 Walt Disney Music Company (ASCAP)
Produced by Matthew Gerrard

What I've Been Looking For (Reprise)
Written and Produced by Andy Dodd and Adam Watts
© 2005 Walt Disney Music Company (ASCAP)

Breaking Free
Written and Produced by Jamie Houston
© 2005 Walt Disney Music Company (ASCAP)

We're All in This Together
Written by Matthew Gerrard and Robbie Nevil
© 2005 Walt Disney Music Company (ASCAP)
Produced by Matthew Gerrard

This is a Parragon book
First published in 2007
Parragon
Queen Street House
4 Queen Street
Bath, BA1 1HE, UK

ISBN 978-1-4075-0737-8
Manufactured in China
Copyright © 2007 Disney Enterprises, Inc.
℗ 2007 Walt Disney Records
All rights reserved. No part of this publication may be reproduced, stored in a retrieval system, or transmitted by any means, mechanical, photocopying, recording or otherwise, without the prior permission of the copyright holder.

Disney
HIGH SCHOOL MUSICAL

PaRragon

Bath • New York • Singapore • Hong Kong • Cologne • Delhi • Melbourne

At a way-cool winter resort, our East High basketball star, Troy Bolton, was shooting hoops with his dad on this indoor court. But Troy's mother was already dressed for a party when she came to break up the game. Troy's father, who was also our team's coach, had totally forgotten what night it was. I mean, hello! He gave his wife this, like, dead look. "Right, the party … the party. New Year's Eve!" When Coach Bolton went to change for the completely tragic grown-ups party, Mrs Bolton told Troy about what Troy prayed would be an okay teen party downstairs in the Freestyle Club.

In another part of the resort, Gabriella Montez was all curled up with a book, and her mother was having a hissy fit about it because she'd already gone and laid out Gabriella's clothes for the teen party. So she, like, yanked the book from Gabriella's hands. "Enough reading."

"Oh, but Mom, I'm almost done, and …"

Down at the Freestyle Club, there was this awesome Karaoke contest. Two spotlights searched the room for the next unsuspecting victims. One light landed on Troy; the other on Gabriella. As the MC led them to the stage, each of them was just, like – oh my gosh! – but when the music started, they began to sing. And you know what? Their voices were amazing!

When the song was finished the room went insane. Troy and Gabriella were all shy and everything, so they just, like, stared at each other.

"You have an amazing voice. You're a singer, right?"

"That was the first time I've done something like that. I mean it was so cool."

"I know, completely."

"Well, you sounded like you've done a lot of singing, too."

"Yeah, sure, lots. My shower head is very impressed with me."

There was the countdown to midnight and then a way-huge fireworks display. Troy and Gabriella put their pictures and numbers in each others phones. But the next day Troy's family had to leave and he was left wondering if he would ever see his amazing singing partner again.

   Back at East High in Albuquerque, our
homeroom teacher, Ms Darbus, was confiscating cell
phones, dropping them into that little bucket of hers marked
"Cell-itary confinement." It was the first day after winter break,
and Gabriella was a new student. From across the room, Troy
recognized her. Well, the big basketball jock nearly fainted!
He was, like, too blown away to think of Ms Darbus's cell
phone rule, so what do you think he went and did? He called
Gabriella's phone and got them both in trouble. "We have zero
tolerance for cell phones in class. So, we will get to know each
other in detention. Cell phone… and welcome to East High,
Miss Montez."

Outside in the hall, Gabriella and Troy were ecstatic to have found each other again. "I can't believe you live here. I looked for you at the lodge on New Year's Day, but ..."

"... I know, we had to leave first thing."

Gabriella soon discovered that as the school's leading jock, Troy was way-embarrassed about that New Year's Eve duet. "It was ... cool. But, you know, my friends – it's, uh, it's not what I do. That was like a ... a different person."

In the lobby, our two love birds (Okay, they didn't know it yet, but I'm like, hello!), well, they saw the bulletin for the winter musical. It was directed by the dreaded Ms Darbus, who was also the drama teacher. Troy smiled. "Oh, now that you've met Ms Darbus, I'll bet you just can't wait to sign up for that."

Just then, Sharpay, who was this total clotheshorse and who was, like, totally in love with herself – though she did have perfect nail beds – anyway, Sharpay goes and covers all of the empty spaces on the sign-in sheet with her gi-normous autograph. "Oh, were you going to sign up, too? My brother and I have starred in all the school's productions, and we really welcome newcomers. There are a lot of supporting roles in the show."

In the school gym that day, Troy and his friend Chad were taking turns guarding each other. But Troy's mind was not where it should have been: like, on basketball practice? "So dude, you know that school musical thing? Is it true you get extra credit just for auditioning?"

"Who cares?"

Chad's total lack of interest in that wimpy musical was all Troy needed to snap out of it and, like, focus on our big playoff game, right? Finally, he came to his senses and started shouting orders. "All right, Wildcats. Pair up, let's go, run." The East High Wildcats sprang into action. Go Wildcats!

Speaking of games, Sharpay and her brother, Ryan, were getting all freaked out about Troy and Gabriella eye-balling the audition sign-up sheet, and decided they better keep Gabriella occupied. In a Web search, they learned that she was the smartest student at her other schools. And would you believe it? They faked a note from Gabriella to Taylor, the leader of East High's "brainiacs", asking to join the Scholastic Decathlon. Taylor told Gabriella there would totally be a chair open for Gabriella at the Scholastic Decathlon team's first competition that next week. Gabriella was like, huh?

On the day of the big auditions, Troy told Chad he had too much homework to make it to work out with the team, but that was a total lie. Troy wanted to go to the auditions. And when he got there, do you know what he did? He hid behind a mop in the back of the theatre! At the piano there was this nerdy little four-eyed girl named Kelsi, who like, wrote the whole musical. Ms Darbus was busy being her bossy self. "This is where the true expression of the artist is realized, where inner truth is revealed through the actor's journey, where … was that a cell phone?"

Kelsi said the noise was not a cell phone. It was, like… the recess bell? Hello? Ughh!

Troy was amazed at how tragic the students that auditioned
were and at the snippy way Ms Darbus told them to get lost.
Out of nowhere, Gabriella was standing in the dark beside
him. "Your friends don't know you're here, right?"

"Right."

"Ms Darbus is a little... harsh."

"The Wildcat superstar is... afraid?"

"No, no, I'm not afraid I... just... scared."

"Me, too."

That was when that stuck up show-off Sharpay and her
goofy brother Ryan took the stage. They had an entire routine
worked out. Gabriella and Troy couldn't believe how out-of-
control glitzy the whole thing was, like some Las Vegas review.

I have to admit, Sharpay and Ryan's performance was awesome. And no one dared try to outdo them. Kelsi, the composer girl, began gathering up her music. She hated what they had done to her song, but she said nothing. Ms Darbus barked out a last call for other auditioners. "Any last-minute sign-ups? No? Good. Done."

She was already leaving the auditorium when Gabriella spoke up. "I'd like to audition, Ms Darbus." But Ms Darbus said she was too late, she'd missed the audition, and anyway, there was no one to sing with her.

That was when Troy stepped forward. "I'll sing with her."

Darbus was, like, in shock. "Troy Bolton? Where's your 'sports posse', or whatever it's called?"

"Team. But I'm here alone. Actually, I'm here to sing with her."

Ms Darbus kept heading for the exit. It was too late for Gabriella and Troy to sing. Just then, Kelsi got up from the piano. And you know what? She totally tripped! Her music flew everywhere. Troy leapt to her assistance. "So why are you so afraid of Ryan and Sharpay? Without you, there is no show. You're the playmaker here, Kelsi."

Kelsi's face was all lit up. "Do you want to hear how the duet is supposed to sound?"

As the composer girl began to play, she pushed the music across the piano to Troy. He and Gabriella looked at it, and then they began to sing.

When they were through, Ms Darbus appeared at the back of the theatre, where she'd been hiding out and listening all along. "Bolton, Montez, you have a callback. Kelsi, give them the duet from the second act. Work on it with them."

The next day, Sharpay saw the callback notice on the lobby bulletin board. "Callback!"

She totally wigged out, while her brother Ryan – who, if you want to know the truth, was kind of a doofus – just looked confused. A big crowd of kids ran over to see what Sharpay's problem was. With them came Chad and his fellow Wildcats, Jason and Zeke. The boys were disgusted to see Troy's name on the callbacks for the musical.

And then things got, like, really bizarre. With Troy's big secret out in the open, lunch period was just plain strange. The skaterdudes, jocks, brainiacs and cheerleaders were all at their own tables. Then, this very tall jock named Zeke made an outrageous confession. He said he loved to bake. A jock who likes to bake? And then this total brainiac named Martha said hip hop music was her secret passion. Even a skaterdude gave it up. He said he played the cello. The cello? I'm like, what-ever! It seemed as if all the kids at East High had another side to them. So I guess it's true – you can't always tell a book by its cover. Me? When I'm not busy with the squad, I'm into quantum physics.

Gabriella walked in with a tray in her hands. Suddenly she, like, stumbled! Oopsy! The chili fries on her tray went sailing and landed – right on Sharpay! Gabriella tried to wipe the mess from Sharpay's blouse with a napkin, but it only made it worse. She apologized all over the place, and ran away upset. Sharpay was, like, scary angry by the time Ms Darbus came by. "What is going on here?"

"Look at this! That Gabriella girl just dumped her lunch on me ... on purpose! It's all part of their plan to ruin our musical." Sharpay pointed one of her flawless nail beds at the jock table. "And Troy and his basketball robots are obviously behind it. Why do you think he auditioned?"

When Troy saw the commotion between Gabriella and Sharpay, he tried to help. Chad stopped him. He led Troy over to the jocks table and gestured around the room. "Do you see what's happening here, man? Our team is coming apart because of your singing thing. Even the drama geeks and brainiacs suddenly think that they can … talk to us. Suddenly people think they can do … other stuff. They've got you thinking show tunes, when we've got a playoff game next week."

Ms Darbus was beyond furious. She went stomping into Coach Bolton's office. "Your all-star son turned up at my audition. Now, I give every student an even chance … but if he is planning some sort of a practical joke in my chapel of the arts …"

"Troy doesn't even sing."

"Oh, well, you're wrong about that. But I will not allow my *Twinkle Towne* musical to be made into a farce."

"*Twinkle Towne?*"

"See! I knew it! I knew it!"

Gabriella got a note from Troy asking her to meet him in the horticulture club garden – which was like, on the roof of the school. "So this is your private hideout?" Troy told her he just wanted to be ordinary, not 'the basketball guy'. Gabriella said she didn't want to be known just as 'freaky math girl' anymore, either. "So you really want to do the callbacks?"

"Hey, just call me 'freaky callback boy'."

Those two wacked kids began rehearsing their duet for the callback audition. They spent like a bezillion hours working with Composer Girl, which made Troy late for basketball practice. And that made Coach Bolton really peeved.

So Chad and the jocks decided to take matters into their own hands. It was time to get Troy away from that Gabriella girl and the singing. They went to the chemistry lab and met with Taylor and the scholastic club, who agreed to help. Here's what happened: First, the jocks gave Troy a pep talk, which they got on video. The talk tricked Troy into saying things he, like, didn't really mean. "... the singing thing is nothing ... Gabriella is not important. I'll forget about her, I'll forget the audition, and we'll go out and get that championship."
On a laptop, Taylor and her club showed Gabriella the video of Troy. The poor thing. She was, like, totally crushed!

Gabriella told Troy she didn't want to do the callbacks either. Troy was confused. And you know what? It was sad, because from then on, he just wasn't himself around school – and neither was poor little Gabriella. Chad and the jocks felt bad about it. They went to the roof garden to find Troy. "We had a meeting about how we haven't been acting like a team." Over in the chemistry lab, Taylor was confessing the secret plan to Gabriella.

Later that evening, Troy showed up at Gabriella's house. He told her how he really felt – and he did it with the song they were going to do for the audition. Gabriella smiled. They were back in the game!

Snooping around as usual, Sharpay and Ryan got wind of how good Troy and Gabriella sounded and you'll never believe what they did.

They convinced Ms Darbus that Troy and Gabriella were a threat to the show, and got her to reschedule the auditions for the same time as Troy's playoff and Gabriella's decathlon. Boy, were they heartbroken when they saw that the callback time had been changed. Luckily, Taylor's computer and science expertise came to the rescue: the playoff ended when the scoreboard went, like, totally haywire, and the decathlon was cut short when a vial of chemicals overheated and stunk up the room. Eew!

Troy and Gabriella ran like heck to the auditorium, but it was too late. Ms Darbus was already 'concluding'. "Congratulations to all, the cast list will be posted."

"No, wait! Wait, Ms Darbus, wait. We're ready. We can sing."

Then like magic, half the school materialized and started to pour in. Kelsi started to play and Gabriella and Troy took the microphones. At first,

Gabriella was scared. It was just too weird having all those people staring at her. But Troy put her at ease.

It was awesome! In the back of the auditorium stood Coach Bolton. He'd never heard his son sing before and was he ever proud.

With the scoreboard working again, the Wildcats won the playoffs. Go team! Wildcats rock! It seemed like the entire school had gone, like, completely wack. The band took to the court and all the students were singing and dancing along.

Chad presented Troy with the game ball, but Troy turned right around and gave it to that mousy little composer girl, Kelsi – who shook her hair out and you know what? She wasn't so mousy anymore. Even her nail beds were perfect. "Composer, here's your game ball. You deserve it … playmaker."